SAM and JUMP

Jennifer K. Mann

CANDLEWICK PRESS

This is Sam—and Jump.

They do everything together.

Because they are best friends.

One day, they went to the beach . . .

where they met Thomas.

Sam and Thomas played all day.

And, when it was time for Sam to leave,
they promised to play again tomorrow.

Sam fell asleep in the car, but when they were almost home, he awoke with a jolt: Jump!

But it was too dark to go back.

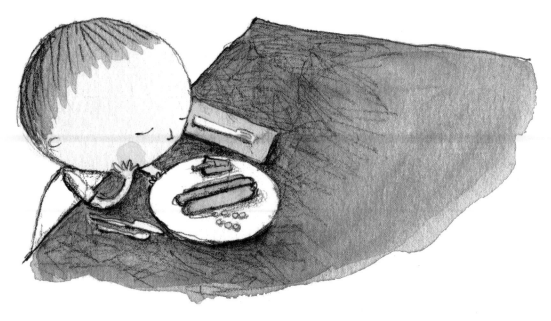

Sam could not
eat his dinner.

Even a bedtime
story didn't help.

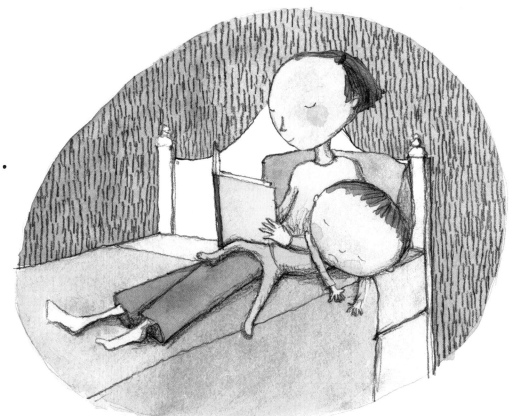

"Don't worry," said Mama.
"We'll look for Jump
in the morning."

But Sam couldn't help thinking about all the things that might have happened to Jump.

Early the next morning,
Mama drove Sam to the beach.

But Jump was nowhere to be seen.

Nothing was fun without Jump.

Then Thomas arrived.

"Jump!"

Now Sam and Thomas—and
Jump—are best friends.

This one is for my sister, who took me back to the beach to look for my lost doll. And for my dad, who made it possible to be at the beach in the first place.

First edition 2016

Library of Congress Catalog Card Number 2015934466
ISBN 978-0-7636-7947-7

16 17 18 19 20 21 CCP 10 9 8 7 6 5 4 3 2 1

Printed in Shenzhen, Guangdong, China

FSC
www.fsc.org
MIX
Paper from
responsible sources
FSC® C008047

This book was typeset in Providence Sans.
The illustrations were done in watercolor, pencil, and digital magic.

Candlewick Press
99 Dover Street
Somerville, Massachusetts 02144

visit us at www.candlewick.com